The Derbyshire Set ~ Book 9

Regency Historical Romance

Lady Theodoras Christmas Wish

Arietta Richmond

Dreamstone Publishing © 2016

www.dreamstonepublishing.com

ISBN: 1925499375

ISBN-13: 978-1-925499-37-7

Disclaimer

This is a work of fiction. Names, characters, places, organisations, events, and incidents are either products of the author's imagination or used fictitiously.

For everyone who had the grace to be patient while this book, and every other book that I have written, was coming into existence, who provided cups of tea, and food, when the writing would not let me go, and endured countless times being asked for opinions.

For the readers who inspire me to continue writing, by buying my books! Especially for those of you who have taken the time to email me, or to leave reviews, and tell me what you love about these books, and what you'd like to see more of – thank you – I'm listening, I promise to write more about your favourite characters.

For my growing team of beta readers and advance reviewers – it's thanks to you that others can enjoy these books in the best presentation possible!

And for all the writers of Regency Historical Romance, whose books I read, who inspired me to write in this fascinating period.

Books by Arietta Richmond

His Majesty's Hounds

Claiming the Heart of a Duke
Intriguing the Viscount
Giving a Heart of Lace
Being Lady Harriet's Hero
Enchanting the Duke
Redeeming the Marquess
Finding the Duke's Heir
Winning the Merchant Earl
Healing Lord Barton
Kissing the Duke of Hearts
Loving the Bitter Baron
Falling for the Earl
Rescuing the Countess
Betting on a Lady's Heart
Attracting the Spymaster
Courting a Spinster for Christmas
Restoring the Earl's Honour
From Soldier Spy to Lord (contains the first three books in one volume)
To Love a Determined Lady (Contains Books 4, 5 and 6 in one volume)

A Duke's Daughters – The Elbury Bouquet

A Spinster for a Spy (Lily)
A Vixen for a Viscount (Hyacinth)
A Bluestocking for a Baron (Rose) (coming soon)
A Diamond for a Duke (Camellia) (coming soon)
A Minx for a Merchant (Primrose) (coming soon)
An Enchantress for an Earl (Violet) (coming soon)
A Maiden for a Marquess (Iris) (coming soon)
A Heart for an Heir (Thorne) (coming soon)

The Regency Scandals Series

The Gift of a Christmas Scandal

Lady Mariel's Scandalous Love (coming soon)

Christmas with *That* Duke (coming soon)

The Nettlefold Chronicles

The Duke and the Spinster

To Dance with the Dangerous Duke

A Duke in Autumn (coming soon)

A Christmas Bride for the Duke (coming soon)

The Derbyshire Set

A Gift of Love (Prequel short story)

A Devil's Bargain (Prequel short story - coming soon)

The Earl's Unexpected Bride

The Captain's Compromised Heiress

The Viscount's Unsuitable Affair

The Count's Impetuous Seduction

The Rake's Unlikely Redemption

The Marquess' Scandalous Mistress

A Remembered Face (Bonus short story – coming soon)

The Marchioness' Second Chance

A Viscount's Reluctant Passion

Lady Theodora's Christmas Wish

The Duke's Improper Love (coming soon)

A Gentleman's Unconventional Courtship (coming soon)

The Derbyshire Set, Omnibus Edition, Volume 1 (the first three books in one volume.)

The Derbyshire Set, Omnibus Edition, Volume 2 (the second three books in one volume.)

Other Books

The Scottish Governess

Her Summer Duke

The Earl's Reluctant Fiancée (coming soon)

The Crew of the Seadragon's Soul Series, (coming soon - a set of 10 linked novels)

Chapter One

"Ouch!"

Lady Theodora's voice was sharp as she exclaimed at the sudden pain. She got no sympathy from Polly, her maid. Polly was used to her young mistress, and simply sighed.

"Miss, if you could just sit still while I finish putting up your hair, it wouldn't get pulled. I do declare, you're more fidgety than young Etta – but at least she has the excuse of being two years old!"

Polly had not yet adapted to calling Theodora 'my Lady' – for it was not all that long since the formal adoption papers had been signed.

Those papers had taken her from being simply 'Miss Theodora Rockingham', the Earl of Stanningfield's ward, to being 'Lady Theodora Rockingham', the Earl of Stanningfield's daughter.

Theodora herself was not yet used to it, although it was delightful to be able to call the Earl 'papa' after so long. It had been, in a way, his present to her for her 17th birthday – the finalisation of the adoption process.

And, that afternoon, she had been given yet more wonderful news – it had been a truly amazing few months!

For that afternoon she had been told that not only was there to be a Christmas Ball at Havisham Hall, but that she would be permitted to attend, as an adult! It would be the first Christmas Ball held there since the old Earl's passing, some 8 years or more ago.

Theodora wanted nothing so much as to rush down to dinner, so that she could sooner ask for more details of the Ball, but the sting of her pulled hair, and Polly's patient admonition, made her try very hard to stop fidgeting and wait – after all, if she was to be treated as an adult (finally!), it was best that she act like it – at least enough that Polly did not compare her to baby Etta!

Once she sat still, allowing her mind to drift off into fairy-tale imaginings of how the Ball might be, populated, of course, with handsome gentlemen who quite fell in love with her on the spot, Polly had her hair untangled and all pinned up in no time.

Once it was done Theodora stood, and looked at herself in the mirror. Her dress was new, for she had entirely grown out of all of her old clothes, so another part of her birthday delights had been the ordering of a whole new wardrobe. And these clothes were definitely those of a fairly fashionable young Lady, not a child.

She was amazed at what Polly could do with her mass of rich dark brown hair, taming it into intricate, yet delicate coils, which almost glowed in the light, with glints of red and gold as the natural highlights shone through. The dress she wore was a pale rose gold colour – perfectly setting off her hair, without being too strong a colour for a young woman.

She almost didn't recognise herself!

The stillness did not last long though – she had never been one to sit quietly by – Theodora was more likely to be found in the stables, or running about in the grounds, given the chance, than sitting demurely with embroidery.

She whirled, the artful tendrils of her hair lifting, like the skirt of the dress, with the force of her movement, as the excitement took hold again, and, laughing in delight at the sensation, went down to dinner.

Chapter Two

Etta ran around and around the nursery, pushing a wooden train, and making her best imitation of train noises – which was a little difficult, as trains were so new, that she, like most people, had never actually seen a real one. Such minor issues did not concern her. At 2 years old, Etta was secure in her world, and was quite able to deal with imagining the train to be real, no matter what.

Eddie, just one year old, did not have any concerns – he sat happily on the rug in front of Theodora, gurgling and laughing, simply because Etta was laughing, and Theodora was rolling a ball to him.

Theodora was having a hard time concentrating on playing with the children, even though she usually adored doing so. Her mind kept drifting away into thoughts of the coming Ball. In just a few weeks, the house would be full of guests, the Ballroom decorated and brilliantly lit, and she would be amongst it all!

"Tia, Tia!"

Eddie demanded her attention, holding out his little hands for the ball. Eddie had just begun to talk, and, like Theodora herself, at that age, could not manage to say 'Theodora' – so Tia it was. Hearing it still shook Theodora's composure - for she had not been called Tia for more than 4 years, since Gran died. To hear it in the child's voice was bittersweet – it brought back all the sad memories, even though the children were a delight.

And now, she thought with satisfaction, they were officially her brother and sister! She rolled the ball again, then obeyed Etta's command to watch her, and applaud the train's speed, but was soon lost in thoughts of the Ball again.

For surely there would be handsome gentlemen there. Gentlemen that she had not met.

Gentlemen who would dance with her, who would, she most intensely hoped, fall in love with her at first sight. Of course, it would also be delightful if she fell in love with one of them.....

She wanted romance, wanted love, wanted, oh so very much, all those things that her mother had not had. She pushed that part of the thought away, and went back to imagining herself swept away to dance with a handsome man, wooed, and even kissed. Whatever that might feel like – she was certain that it would be wonderful.

Eddie tugged at her hand, wanting her attention again, and Tia (for, inside, that was how she still thought of herself) turned to him, smiling. In that moment, it occurred to her that she would like to have children of her own one day. Which would definitely require a handsome gentleman to fall in love with!

She silently vowed to herself that one day she would – and that she would make sure that their childhood was very different from hers (for whilst she had been loved, always, she had not had the circumstances or the money for much more than just love).

The desire to see her own children, and for them to be as happy and carefree as Eddie and Etta, was an ache of such intensity that it surprised her.

Her musings were interrupted when Etta, having become utterly over exuberant, tripped on the ball that Eddie had just rolled, and collapsed in a crying heap, tangled with the wooden train. Gathering her to her with calming words, Theodora resolved that she would think more, later, about what it might be like to have a child of her own.

Chapter Three

Catherine, Countess of Stanningfield, looked up from the list that lay on her small writing desk in the informal parlour. She started out through the terrace doors across the winter gardens, letting the pen drop from her fingers to the side of the paper.

She was quite sure that she had forgotten someone who should be invited. She had not, before now, realised quite how difficult it would be to formulate a guest list for the grand occasion of the first Christmas Ball at Havisham House since Charles had become Earl.

The matter of her own, somewhat lowly, origins made choosing guests even harder.

For she would wish her mother to attend, and, although her mother had become used to mingling with some of the nobility on occasion, she was still not entirely comfortable with many. Charles' wide circle of acquaintance, and complex tangle of family, meant that he would wish a large contingent to be invited. And then there were those of the *ton* who must be invited (even though many would not make the journey, as winter was making the roads less and less pleasant to travel).

But for Theodora's sake, they must be invited. If she was to be launched in the coming London season, she must meet as many people now, as possible, to ensure that she was accepted, and that no touch of scandal or question of her heritage might tarnish her opportunities in life.

As if the thought had summoned her, Theodora tapped on the door and entered, followed by Charles. Catherine smiled in genuine pleasure, delighted by how beautiful Theodora looked.

Charles came to Catherine and bent to kiss her lightly. They had been married three years now, but were still as delighted in each other as they had been at the start.

Catherine sighed, looking up at Charles.

"This list is becoming huge, and yet I am still not sure that I have remembered everyone who should be invited! If they all choose to attend, I've no idea where we will put them all – the house will be overflowing, and so will the Inn in Harteston, and perhaps the Inn in Lavenham too!"

Charles laughed at her worried expression.

"My dear Catherine, I am certain that the innkeepers will be most pleased with us, if we bring them customers! And we will manage to squeeze many of those closest to us in here, never fear. For now, let's go through the list together, and make sure that all of 'the important people' are on it."

Theodora, who had been standing to one side, surreptitiously trying to read the list that lay in front of Catherine, could not contain her enthusiasm.

"Oh yes, please, can we do that? I want to know all about everyone who will be here!"

Charles and Catherine shared a smile at her reaction. Charles and Theodora sat, and Catherine passed the list to Charles. He sat quietly, reading through it, muttering as he did, much to Theodora's annoyance.

She forced herself to sit still, at least for the first few minutes.

She knew that well behaved young ladies did not leap up and lean over people's shoulders to read what they were reading. It was a very tempting idea, though....

After a few minutes, Charles and Catherine began to discuss names – some that Theodora recognised, like Viscount Bellham and his wife, the Marquess of Hemsbridge (whose marriage had caused quite a scandal), the Earl of Derbyshire, his daughters, and their husbands, and a number of others. Then they strayed into names that she had not heard before.

It would be quite an exalted company, from the sound of it, with so many titled and wealthy people. But.... Theodora still did not know which of the names that she was hearing were those of unmarried and eligible gentlemen...

"But papa," she asked "who are these people you are mentioning? Please, won't you tell me about them?"

"Well," Charles paused, looking at her with barely repressed amusement, "Am I correct in assuming that what you really want to know is which gentlemen attending might be young and handsome?"

Theodora blushed, but had the good grace to be honest and nod, acknowledging the truth of his words.

"There are at least 15 eligible gentlemen on this list, although a few of them are perhaps rather old from your point of view. The most eligible is Chase Harringdon, the Duke of Montford. He only recently came into the title, somewhat unexpectedly, when his great-uncle died without an heir. Mind you, I'm not at all sure that you should be looking at him, he has rather a rakish reputation, not to mention being, at nearly 30, somewhat older than I might like for you. Everyone thought him unlikely to marry, with his brother his heir for the Marquessate, but, now that he is the Duke, and his brother the Marquess, he will need to marry, and get himself an heir."

Theodora said nothing, her mind already floating off into excited imaginings again.

A Duke! And 30 was not so old, if he was handsome. She pushed aside any concern about the idea of a rakish reputation, finding it, in the manner common to fanciful young girls who were just out of the schoolroom, rather more exciting than not.

The Earl had continued speaking, naming another three gentlemen who might be of interest to a young lady, but Tia did not hear a word of it, she was so lost in her imaginings.

Over the next hour, after much discussion, the guest list was finalised, and the arduous task of writing out all those invitations begun.

Tia was drawn out of her dreaming and recruited to help Catherine with the writing, for she had a fair hand. Crafting beautiful writing was, Catherine reflected, one of the few parts of her schooling that Theodora had actually enjoyed – for the most part, she had been more interested in playing with the kittens in the stables than in learning anything of use about the world.

Chapter Four

With the invitations all sent, and acceptances flowing in, the next few weeks became a whirlwind of preparation, with the staff continually calling on Catherine and Charles for decisions and instruction, as vast quantities of food were ordered, decorations arranged, an orchestra engaged, and the thousand and one small essential details involved in providing accommodation and food for a horde of house guests addressed.

With decorations being progressively placed throughout the house, it was starting to feel like Christmas, Christmas as Tia had never seen it before, and her excitement increased every day, until she was living at fever pitch.

Somehow, between helping where she could, and spending time with the children (for, whilst their nurse, Mrs Millwood, was a truly wonderful woman, she did need to rest sometimes, and the children truly missed Tia if they did not see her, and spend time with her, every day), she still found time to dream, in a few quiet moments here and there. Those dreams featured, usually, a handsome Duke, who swept her off her feet, danced with her, kissed her hand (or maybe more!), and singled her out for his attentions in a most satisfactory way.

Those dreams also, a little to her shame when she considered it, often featured the few female acquaintances of the nobility that Tia could claim – featured them watching her with envy. For, as the ward of the Earl of Stanningfield, she had been, always, neither one thing not the other – not really of the *ton*, like the other girls were, nor really of the lesser classes. Stuck in between, Tia had been tolerated, but not really accepted, not drawn into their close friendship. They had been all too ready to speak of her disparagingly, if only to make themselves feel more confident in their superiority.

Chide herself as she might, she could not but enough the thought of their discomfiture now.

If nothing else, even if she did not catch the attention of a handsome and eligible gentleman, with the formal adoption as Charles and Catherine's daughter, she was officially of their class, and it would be much harder for them to ignore her now.

A few might even welcome her, which would be considerably more pleasant than dealing with the few who would still disregard her as much as they felt they could, without directly offending the Earl.

On her way to the nursery, Tia passed the ballroom doors, just as the footmen exited, after having put in place yet more decorations. She couldn't resist quickly taking a look. Slipping through the doors, she found the room empty, just for now.

The vast space was transformed by the elegant cloth drapes that had been hung all around, and the huge decorative urns and vases that stood all around, waiting to hold festive greenery and hothouse flowers on the night of the Ball.

The chandeliers shone, with every crystal having been polished, and she envisaged how wonderful the room would look, with all of the candles lit, and sparkling traces of light scattered across the rich drapes.

Imagining the orchestra in place, and the room full or swirling dancers, Tia could not resist – she closed her eyes, humming the music of a scandalous waltz softly, and danced around the room, imagining herself to be in the arms of a handsome Duke, who had eyes only for her. The trailing curls of her hair escaped, as always, from their pins, lifted with her movement, the light fabric of her favourite day dress swirled around her ankles, and, for that few moments at least, her life was transformed.

An odd thump noise startled her out of the beautiful vision, and she stopped, wobbling inelegantly, as she spun towards the door, just in time to see the footmen hauling another large marble urn into the room.

"Our apologies Lady Theodora – there's no damage – it just slipped a bit, and Tom here thumped into the wall. But we've got it now."

She smiled, assuring them that she was not concerned, and went on her way to the nursery, happy that they had not seen her dancing about like a mad thing, all alone in the Ballroom.

But she didn't regret doing it. If the real Ball felt as wonderful as those few moments had......

Tia's obsession with the coming Ball only increased, as the days went by. She would tell herself not to be silly, that the Duke might be ugly, or look old and fat, or, having been a rake for some years, might be worn, cynical and uninterested in unsophisticated young ladies, but part of her was utterly stubborn, and would not let go of her dreams.

She danced about the house whenever she could, she danced the children around the nursery floor, much to their delight, she told them stories of princesses and heroes, and, all the while, she came, more and more, to realise how desperately she wanted to meet someone special.

For some time now, Tia had been feeling rather out of sorts, and had not really known why. But now she did – she was grown, yet she had not really been an adult. She was no longer a child, but had no life of her own as an adult.

She loved papa and Catherine very much, but…. They were still, only three years into their marriage, very caught up in each other, and their new children. It had left Tia feeling somehow excess. She wanted someone of her own – someone to feel about her, as papa so obviously felt about Catherine.

Someone that she could love like that too.

The more that she thought about it, the stronger it became, until, one day, yet again standing in the Ballroom, she closed her eyes, and made a wish, a Christmas wish. For this Christmas, she would like a very special gift.

She wished that, at the Ball, on the eve of Christmas, she would meet someone special, someone who could give her that life and love that she wanted, someone to marry, and have children with. She wished for a sign. She wished that, if she met the right person at the Ball, she would know – know because he would kiss her, she who had never been kissed....

The intensity of the wishing took her breath away, left her heart aching in her chest. It would happen – she was sure of it!

Chapter Five

Theodora glared at the dress that Polly was holding up for her. The bed was covered with other dresses, as were the chairs in the room. And she wasn't happy with any of them. Choosing what to wear was so difficult!

It had to be just perfect, for this, her first Ball!

She took a deep breath, and valiantly resisted the urge to throw a foot stamping, screaming tantrum from frustration. She was an adult now. She had to remember that.

Closing her eyes, she imagined, again, that she was dancing with a handsome Duke.

In the imagined scene she cast her eyes down, trying to see what she wore. All she got was a faint impression of colour, but it was enough for her to know, instantly, which dress to choose.

Opening her eyes, she went to the bed, and carefully extracted one dress from the pile. It was a pale ivory dress, with an overlay of delicate golden tissue lace. It almost glowed from the soft gold, and she knew that it made all of the highlights in her hair glow as well. It was decorated, tastefully, minimally, at the bodice and hem, with some tiny clusters of red rosebuds with intense green leaves, all made of silk. The red drew the eye, and the green made her brilliant green eyes seem even more so.

It was pale and demure enough to not offend those who thought that young ladies shouldn't wear anything of strong colour, but interesting enough to be different from all of those insipid white dresses she saw illustrated in the fashion journals (when any of those managed to reach them, all the way from London). It was also elegant in its simplicity – no massive flounces and frills for her.

It was exactly what she wanted.

Polly nodded in approval of her choice, and patiently started putting all of the other dresses away.

It was immediately obvious what jewellery she should wear with that dress too – Papa (how wonderful it was to finally be able to call him that!) had given her a pearl set on her birthday – a necklace of pearls with tiny gold drops between them, two strings of pearls for twining in the hair, and a matching bracelet. They would suit the dress wonderfully.

Theodora sighed, utterly relieved, as Polly carefully took the dress away to make certain that it was clean and perfectly pressed, for the Ball was in two days' time, on Christmas Eve. She settled in the comfortable chair in front of the window, and stared out at the grounds, where a light dusting of snow decorated the evergreen hedges of the maze and the leafless branches of the trees stood out stark against the winter grey sky.

She had never liked winter much, but this year was different, for with winter had come her birthday, the Ball, and the chance to meet eligible gentlemen.

Remembering her wish, she allowed herself to dream again, picturing herself in the beautiful dress, dancing with a handsome man. He would be tall, strong, with dark hair and piercing eyes. She could not quite imagine his face, but everything else was quite clear. Relaxing, the daydream stayed with her, as she drifted into a doze in the chair

Polly found her there, sleeping, curled like a kitten against the cushions, with a smile on her face, when she came to help Theodora dress for dinner.

Chapter Six

Theodora fidgeted on the stool, nervous and eager in equal measures, as Polly gave a long-suffering sigh and tried her best to get Theodora's hair in place, without jabbing her with the pins as she wriggled.

At last, it was done, and Tia stood, looking at herself in the full-length cheval mirror. It did not look like her. Where had this poised and polished looking lady come from? Polly was a miracle worker, as was the modiste who had crafted the dress.

Impulsively, she spun around and startled Polly by kissing her cheek, afraid to hug her in case she crushed the dress.

"Thank you! I have no idea how you make my hair stay in place like that!"

Taking a deep breath, Theodora left the room, and, feeling like a princess in a story, walked slowly down the stairs. Charles and Catherine, both in immaculate and beautiful evening wear, waited at the bottom, ready to greet the guests once they began to arrive.

Watching Tia descend, Charles barely suppressed a gasp. He was full of pride in his daughter, but, at that moment, she looked so like Monique that it was a bittersweet joy to see her so. Catherine watched him, then turned to watch Theodora, her heart full of love for both of them. This was a wonderful moment.

She reached the bottom of the stairs and smiled, a little shaky still, but full of excitement, which bid to break free at any moment. She was afraid to let it do so, for surely she would completely ruin the impression of an elegant and composed young lady if she spun wildly about the hall for the joy of it!

Catherine took her hand, the sparkle in her eyes hinting at the fact that she had guessed Tia's thoughts, and drew her forward. Just as she did, there came the sound of carriage wheels on the gravel, and then a knock at the door.

"Come, it is time for us to greet our guests."

The Earl placed Catherine's other hand on his arm, and led them both forward, as Wilton opened the door, and ushered the first guests inside.

~~~~~

Well over an hour later, the flow of arrivals finally slowed. Tia thought that every Inn for many miles would be full tonight and the next few nights, she had never seen so many people in the one place at the same time before!

Her feet hurt from standing in the one place, and her face ached from smiling at all of the guests as she had greeted each one. But most of all, her heart ached.

For, whilst there were a few somewhat appealing gentlemen, most were married. Those who were not, were either old, rather ugly, or rather unpleasant — some in ways that she could not entirely define, but which made her not even want to allow them to take her hand in greeting.

Annoyingly, those who did not make her want to flinch away mostly seemed to barely notice her.
~~~~~

As if being now officially the Earl's daughter, and being seventeen, made no difference. She hated feeling invisible!

Most significantly of all, there was, as yet no Duke, handsome or otherwise. Tia could feel her dreams crumbling away inside. Perhaps her wish had been foolish, childish. Was this what being an adult was about? Having to be polite to boring people, whilst inside everything fell apart? It would seem that there was no chance of her wish coming true.

They were about to turn away and go into the ballroom to mingle with the guests, when the sound of one more carriage on the drive reached their ears. The Earl stopped, sighed, and patiently waited for the butler to show the late arrival in. Tia shifted from foot to foot, wanting to move, to ease the ache in her feet – standing in the one spot on a marble floor was painful after a while.

The door opened, and Wilton announced, in his most pompous voice (which usually made Tia want to laugh) "His Grace, the Duke of Montford."

Tia's head snapped up, her eyes sought the newcomer, and, instantly, her evening was restored. For the man who was walking towards them was everything she had imagined, and more.

Now, she thought, blushing, she had a face to put to the man in her dreams.

The Duke was looking at her, as he approached, and she was certain that he could see her blush — which realisation only made her blush more. His eyes caught hers, and she could not have looked away if she wanted to. They were deep brown eyes, with a faint gold light in them, like the touch of sunlight on the best German velvet. She quite fell into them, forgetting her surroundings for a moment.

She forced herself to look away, for staring was the height of rudeness. Her eyes slid from his, noting the angled planes of his cheeks, and the curve of a smile on his lips, the strong chin below them, before coming to rest on his hand, as it reached out to take hers.

He bowed over her hand, placing a kiss on it, a kiss which lasted just a little longer than was proper, before standing straight again, a full smile lighting his face at her confusion.

"Enchanted, my Lady."

His voice was as rich and dark as his eyes, so resonant that she felt it on her skin, as well as hearing it with her ears.

Most amazingly, she thought, it sounded as if he actually meant it, rather than simply delivering the expected words.

He was, she realised, a little older than she had expected, even given Papa's description of him, but the age sat well on him. He had not run to fat from an excess of indulgence, as so often happened to those who led the life of a rake and libertine.

She realised that she was woolgathering again, and that he knew, and was amused. Blushing, she spoke, knowing that she had been silent too long.

"Welcome, Your Grace." She curtsied, elegant and practiced (and very, very glad of that practice now), and he released her hand, moving on to speak to Catherine.

∾∾∾∾∾

Chase was more shaken that he wanted to admit. He had quite forgotten, until it came time to greet the Countess, that he still had hold of the girl's hand. She was a pretty enough chit, and certainly more pleasant to look on that the silly girls that the matchmaking mamas of the *ton* kept thrusting at him.

But that was no reason to forget himself – it wouldn't do to seem too interested in any girl, no matter how small his actions, or the gossip would be marrying him off. He most definitely wasn't ready for that!

Anyway, this one was barely out of the schoolroom – he had always liked his women rather more sophisticated and experienced than the average young Lady of the *ton*. He had to admit though, he could no longer hold to his determination not to marry. The Dukedom needed an heir. He pushed the though aside, finished his greetings, and turned, with his hosts, to go into the Ballroom.

∿∿∿∿∿

Catherine had watched the interaction between Theodora and the Duke with some amusement – she suspected that Theodora was smitten.

Which may well be a good thing, so long as it did not go too far. Theodora was a dreamer, she was a girl made for romance, for activity and adventure, not for sitting quietly by and being bland in the way that was usually expected of the young ladies of the *ton*.

And Catherine was glad of it, where many mothers might not be. For her own mother had been scandalous in her time, and Catherine and Charles' marriage had also been rather dramatic and touched with scandal.

They were none the worse for it, and she was quite sure that love was worth it. Let Theodora find her own way, so long as she was not trapped into anything she did not want. Catherine would watch, and protect, but she would never try to lock the girl away.

The Duke was a bit of a surprise. She had not seen him for a year or so, since the wedding of James Blackwood, who was now Viscount Weirton, (his great uncle having finally expired of his longstanding illness) when the Duke had still been the Marquess of Travers, and had stood up with Blackwood at the wedding. Then, he had been a confirmed bachelor, with a history of dissolute and rakish behaviour to rival Blackwood's. It would seem that becoming the Duke had reformed him rather.

Or perhaps it was the effect of seeing Blackwood a changed man, and happy for it? Whatever the cause, he looked fitter, steadier, and more handsome as a result.

~~~~~

Meanwhile Tia was finding herself, now that she had been released from the duty of receiving guests, rather overwhelmed by the flock of gentlemen who vied for her attention.

It seemed that her dance card would be full, but she was having some difficulty in arranging things to ensure that those she did *not* want to dance with were not deeply offended. It became easier when she realised that there were more gentlemen than dances.

But... he had not joined the throng – how could her dream happen, her wish come true, if he did not dance with her? She had no more time to consider, as the orchestra struck up with the tune for a well-known country dance, and the gentleman who had claimed her swept her away to the floor.

Three dances later, she was beginning to see that dancing so much could be exhausting, but that conversing with some of these gentlemen as she danced was even more so. She fanned herself vigorously, glad of the short break between dances, but beginning to be annoyed with the press of gentlemen.
~~~~~

Tia was, however, rather pleased to see that those young ladies who had most scorned her company in the past were looking most envious now, as the eligible men flocked to her. At least that part of her dream had come true (however poor spirited of her it had been to wish it).

Glancing away, wishing something, anything to look at except Viscount Albemarle's spotty face, as he rambled on in an insipid attempt to flatter her, she looked past his shoulder, to discover the Duke watching her, from across the room. For a moment, again, their eyes locked, and Viscount Albemarle's rather grating voice faded away, and it seemed that there was nothing, and no-one, in the room, but her, and the Duke.

Chapter Seven

"Lady Theodora?" Viscount Albemarle's irritating voice brought her back to awareness. It seemed obvious that he had been attempting to get her attention for some time. "Are you quite well?"

She fanned herself even more vigorously before replying. "Why yes, my Lord, I was simply overcome by the warmth for a moment – it is such a crush! "

Albemarle seemed reassured, and Tia wondered briefly what he had been saying. But those thoughts were almost immediately interrupted, when an unexpected voice spoke.

"I believe you promised me this dance, Lady Theodora?"

It was him! The Duke of Montford stood before her, having somehow caused the crush of her admirers to step back a little. He extended his hand, waiting for her to react. As if in her dream, she took the offered hand, smiling.

"Why yes, Your Grace, I believe I did." Theodora spoke, knowing full well that she had done no such thing, but, in that moment, intensely grateful that she had been rescued from the crowd of annoying would-be suitors. And to be rescued in such a manner! It was beyond wonderful.

He placed her hand on his arm, and led her across the room, to the area cleared for dancing. She went, feeling as if she floated, aware, through her glove and his clothing, of the warmth of his arm beneath her fingers, and of the scent of him – a mixture of lemon, something exotic like sandalwood, and something else unidentifiable, yet completely masculine.

It was only as he turned her into his arms that she realised, with complete shock, that the music she heard was a waltz.

Instantly, she knew that all eyes would be on her. At barely seventeen, and not yet officially out, the rules of propriety indicated that she should, most definitely, not be dancing a waltz!

The dance was still regarded as rather scandalous by the older and more conservative members of the *ton* - after all, it brought the lady and gentleman into very close contact, with their bodies almost touching. Startled, Tia looked up at him, to find him watching her, those deep warm eyes filled with amusement, a slight, almost sardonic smile on his sculpted lips. She blushed, instantly. His smile widened.

"Shall we be scandalous, my Lady? Surely you will not be cruel enough to deny me the dance, now that you have escaped the attentions of that flock of young fops?"

There was laughter in his voice, and a challenge. Tia had never been one to refuse a challenge. And, whilst she was, in many ways, wise beyond her years, at that moment she could not bring herself to care one whit about scandal. For this was her dream, only better.

Taking her silence for acquiescence, he began to move, sweeping her into the dance.

They swirled about the floor, and Tia felt even more dreamlike, floating, poised, and balanced, safe and protected in his arms, as they moved effortlessly through the other dancers, almost as if they were alone.

She was still looking deep into his eyes, but could not look away, no matter how terribly forward of her it was. They barely spoke, comfortable in their silence, trapped in each other's' gaze, happily ignoring everyone else.

When she had practiced dancing, learning the steps of the dance from Catherine, she had not realised that it could feel like this.

This was completely different, and so much better than even her imagination could have conjured. Eventually, Tia became aware that the music had ceased, as they swirled to a halt at one side of the room.

The Duke released her, seeming (but perhaps she was imagining it?) reluctant to do so, and bowed over her hand again.

"Thank you, my Lady, that was delightful. Shall I escort you to your father?"

"Why yes, I think that would be best, Your Grace, I fear that my appetite for Viscount Albemarle's conversation is quite sated for now."

Her remark surprised a laugh from him, and another of those brilliant smiles.

When he smiled at her like that, everything else simply disappeared. As he led her across the room, to where Catherine and Charles stood, chatting with some friends, she noticed, again, how many envious eyes followed her, and how much whispering went on behind the fans of the cluster of young ladies near the terrace doors.

Perhaps they really had been scandalous. If so, she would treasure the fact, rather than flinch from it!

The Earl looked up as they approached, and watched them with interest, but made no comment until the Duke had again bowed over her hand, and taken his leave of her.

Then he spoke, quietly. "Was that wise, Theodora? For now you are most certainly going to be an object of scrutiny for all of the more conservative matrons."

Tia was not sure what to say and as she hesitated, Catherine spoke.

"My dear, I do not think that we can chide Theodora for being somewhat unconventional. After all, our wedding was not without scandal."

The Earl smiled at Catherine and took her hand.

"You are quite right my Lady – I am sure that we will all deal with the opinions of others as we must." He turned more to Tia again, and asked "Scandal aside, are you enjoying yourself, child?"

"Oh yes, Papa, it is wonderful! Well... everything except Viscount Albemarle's conversation is wonderful."

Charles and Catherine exchanged another smile at her words – how typical of Theodora! They all stood talking for a short while, before the hopeful young men came to claim Tia for more dancing.

∿∿∿∿∿

Chase was, despite his intentions, finding Lady Theodora interesting. Whilst she seemed, at first glance, simply another fresh young thing, it was obvious that more thought went on in her head than in most young ladies heads. That remark about Albemarle, for example, indicated a quite cutting wit.

He also had to admit that she was stunning.

The simple pale gold gown set her off to perfection – it was actually elegant, rather than a froth of frills like so many young ladies' fashions.

The gold lights in her rich dark hair seemed to echo the colour of the dress, and for one insane moment, he had wanted to pull down all that careful coil of hair and pearls, to bury his hands in the silken softness of it. And her eyes – he had quite fallen into their intense green depths, depths where blue flecks drifted, like the colours of a tropical sea.

For a while, as they danced, he had seen nothing else. Well, nothing else but her lips, he admitted to himself. Lips which he had wanted to kiss. A thought which was overwhelmingly inappropriate in the circumstances. But still, it was tempting.

She had felt good in his arms. He had been quite unable to resist capturing her for that waltz, however scandalous it might have been. And the fact that she chose to be scandalous, rather than cry off, made her all the more interesting. He shook his head – what was he doing, he, the confirmed bachelor, with a rake's reputation and habits, even passingly being interested in a girl barely out of the schoolroom?

Yet he could not get her out of his thoughts. He found himself following her with his eyes, watching her dance another country dance with an over-dandified fop, whose over fussy clothing looked even more so, when contrasted by her understated elegance.

Obviously, he needed to distract himself. He had always found the best distraction from a woman to be another woman, so, resolute, he turned from watching her, and sought out a girl to dance with. They were all watching him, he realised, as he scanned the room, suddenly making him feel as a mouse must, surrounded by cats.

Just for the devilment, he looked for the quietest wallflower there, and found a girl with mousy pale brown hair, in an ill-fitting grey dress, who appeared to be hiding behind some potted greenery near the doors. As he approached her, he was watching, from the corner of his eye, the expressions on the faces of the cluster of more fashionable girls. It was almost enough to make him laugh out loud.

He bowed before the mousy girl, and led her, after she stuttered her shocked agreement, into the dance. As a distraction, he discovered, she was less than satisfactory.

She had no conversation, and, to make matters worse, she almost tripped over her own feet. There was none of the delicious sense of floating effortlessly through the steps that he had felt with Lady Theodora, and, this not being a waltz, he could not even hold her close and support her when she stumbled.

His eyes followed Lady Theodora, no matter his intent not to look for her. Grimly determined, he proceeded to dance with each of the uninteresting girls in turn, until his teeth ached from gritting them together as he forced a socially acceptable smile.

He wanted, more and more, to dance with Lady Theodora again. But that would be taking scandalous just a little too far, and he would not do that to her.

But still, he could not stop himself from watching her.

~~~~~

Tia danced. And danced. And danced. But none of it felt like that waltz with the Duke. By comparison, all other dances were ungainly and awkward.

The gentlemen were either ridiculous, trying to please her with extravagant flattery, or were so self-important that all they could speak of was themselves.

Tia was, to her own surprise, bored by them.

Unintentionally, her eyes sought out the Duke, she somehow could not help herself.
~~~~~

He danced, as was appropriate, with many different ladies, never singling anyone out for too much attention, providing no fodder for gossip, beyond their scandalous waltz. She hated seeing him dance with others, for each time, she was wishing that it was her in his arms, or touching his hand as they passed in the figures of a dance.

But she could not bring herself to look away. Her partners found her distracted, and after some time, she was overcome with the need to get away from them all. If she could not dance with him again, she found that she did not wish to dance at all.

That waltz had felt like her Christmas wish dreams come true, but to now have to watch him with all of the other girls, to have to dance with these other men was just too much to bear. It tarnished her wish and spoiled her dreams.

As the next dance ended, she excused herself from them all, and left the room. She would spend some time in the family parlour – her favourite room - and read, until she could face them all again.

The supper would not be served until after midnight, and she could surely restore her spirits enough to return by then.

The parlour was blessedly quiet, and she sank into her favourite chair with relief, the latest novel in her hand. Annoyingly, she found that she could not settle to reading, her thoughts, instead, replaying, again and again, that waltz.

How it had felt, the look in his eyes, the scent of him, the feel of his arms holding her, the magical way in which they had seemed to float across the floor. It was wonderful…. But…. Her wish had gone further than the dance… and now, she thought, she wanted the rest. Oh so much, so much more even than when she had first wished it.

She ached for it, imagined what it might feel like, for him to hold her again, even closer than in the waltz, imagined what it might feel like to be kissed. For she had never been kissed. The sensible part of her mind said that she was behaving like a wanton.

The part of her that believed in dreams and wishes shoved that thought aside. There was nothing wrong with wishing!

Chapter Eight

Chase released his latest dance partner back to her hopeful looking Mama, and turned away with relief, intending to seek out a drink to fortify himself before selecting the next young lady to torture himself with.

Automatically, he looked for Lady Theodora, and was surprised to see her slip from the room. Frowning, he wondered where she had gone.

A few minutes later, drink in hand, he casually scanned the room again. She wasn't there. It was, of course, none of his business where she was. Perhaps she needed the ladies' retiring room.

Still, he found that he wanted to know.

Downing the drink, he deposited the glass with a passing footman and, before he could think too closely about his actions, left the room through the same door that Lady Theodora had used.

The empty hallway led towards the back of the house, and whilst internally he argued with himself about what he was doing, his feet had no doubts – he proceeded down the hallway, looking for any sign of where she might be.

He felt a bit of a fool, wandering the corridors of a house he didn't know, on the off-chance of finding a girl he shouldn't be looking for, who might not want to see him even if he found her. But he kept walking.

Right at the end of the hallway, a partially ajar door released a strip of light onto the floor – perhaps she was there? Chase slowed as he reached it – what was he doing?

But he kept walking, until he could see, through the partially open door, that it was, indeed, Lady Theodora in the room – alone.

His heart beat faster. He should turn and walk away. She sat in a large armchair, a book on her lap, staring into the fire. He wondered what she was thinking about.

She was beautiful, in a charming, unstudied way. The red gold light from the fire made the gold tissue lace of her dress glitter, and the red and gold tones in her hair echoed the flames. Again, he felt that urge to pull all of the pins from her hair and tangle his hands in it.

Without conscious though, he found himself moving. He stepped quietly through the door, and, just as quietly, shut it behind him. An internal voice screamed at him to get out – for to be found alone with her here would surely result in scandal and marriage.

He ruthlessly silenced the voice, and stepped forward.

∿∿∿∿∿

Tia stared at the flames, unseeing. All she saw, instead, was his face, as he had looked at her when they danced. She had no idea how long she had been sitting there, and she didn't care. This was infinitely more pleasant than dancing with fops and boors.

Then something broke through her dreaming.

A sound?

Perhaps the quiet 'snick' of the door closing?

She turned, feeling still in the dream, and saw him walking across the room towards her. She did not consider the fact that he should not be there, or that she should not be alone with a gentleman. In the dream, it was entirely reasonable, nay utterly desirable, that he be there.

Tia stood, rising smoothly from the chair, the book falling, unnoticed, to the rug at her feet. She walked towards him, her eyes on his, her heart in her eyes. Somehow, she discovered, her hands were reaching for him, and he took them in his, bringing them to his lips. He turned each hand, and kissed her palms, taking her breath away with the sensation, as a heated tingling spread out from the point of each kiss.

He released her hands to fall naturally on his shoulders, and pulled her against him, one hand around her waist, and the other cradling the back of her neck. She went willingly into his embrace, her heart beating hard and her breath coming faster as she felt the hard planes of his body pressed against her softness.

It was her dream – but this was real, at least she thought it was.

And then his head came down to hers, his lips brushed hers, softly at first, then harder, as he deepened the kiss. Tia stilled, unsure, then, as if she had always known how, she began to kiss him in return. His tongue traced the lines of her lips, and she gasped at the sensation, then melted against him as his tongue explored her mouth. Tentatively, she explored his in turn.

Heat rushed through her body, leaving her tingling in ways she had never felt before. It was then that she was certain that this was real, that she had not fallen asleep in the chair, and dreamed of his kiss, but that he was really here, in her arms, kissing her. For there was so much more to the kiss than she had ever imagined. It was beyond what she could have imagined, deliciously, intensely *more*.

His hands slid over her body, gentle caresses, which aroused her, and held her, making her feel wanted, needed, and utterly safe. That this was, in any way, contradictory, did not occur to her.

Eventually, after some unknown length of time, which was both forever, and not long enough, he pulled back from her with a groan. Tia heard a little moan of denial escape her own lips at the loss of his touch.

They stood, still close but no longer touching, simply looking at each other, both, it seemed, stunned by the intensity of their kiss. At almost the same moment, they both become conscious of the fact that they should not be here, alone. But Tia could not speak, she had no compass for a moment like this, and did not want to break the dreamlike state.

"Lady Theodora, it seems I must apologise. That was very wrong of me. But... I cannot say that I am sorry it happened - however inappropriate it may have been." His voice was warm, caressing, and the look in his eyes told her how much he had wanted it – as much as she had, or perhaps, even more.

"Your Grace, I am in agreement. I am not sorry either, although indeed tis most inappropriate."

Tia's eyes sparkled with a sense of mischief he found enchanting, and the fact that she simply agreed with him, rather than instantly screaming 'compromise' and attempting to trap him into marriage was more attractive than anything else she might have done.

His face lit with a smile and, after a moment, he laughed, causing Tia also to burst into laughter. It seemed so silly, that such a wonderful thing should be something to apologise for.

He reached for her hand again, and, bowing over it, as his touch sent waves of tingling warmth through her, kissed her hand slowly, then standing, reluctantly released it as he spoke.

"My Lady, to protect your honour, I will leave you now. But I will, of a certainty, seek your company in a more suitable way tomorrow."

Bowing again, he turned and left the room. Tia thought that perhaps she should have spoken, then realised that it wasn't necessary — for, unquestionably, he knew how she felt.

And that was a remarkable and wonderful thing, all of itself.

∾∾∾∾∾

Chase felt bemused, detached from reality, as if he had stepped into a strange dream. What had he just done? And why? He had always made it a rule not to in any way corrupt innocents, or take advantage of young ladies, lest he end up married to them. Yet he had just voluntarily put himself in a position which could easily have resulted in them being discovered, and forced to marry.

How had he known that she would not reject him, that she would not cry 'compromise'? He had no idea, yet he had been certain. It had seemed dreamlike, completely right. She had just walked into his arms, as if she had been expecting him.

And the kiss had been remarkable, he could not quite define how or why – it had simply been more than any previous kiss in his life. In a situation where he might have been expected to run as fast as he could, congratulating himself on a close escape, he had, instead, truly meant it when he had said that he would seek out her company tomorrow, in a more appropriate manner.

Lady Theodora was an unexpected delight. Beautiful, willing to be unconventional, not, it appeared, interested in gossip or spite, with a sharp wit and an honest open manner. About as opposite from most of the young ladies he was acquainted with as was possible.

For the first time ever, Chase contemplated the idea that, perhaps, a female could be good to be around for more than just physical gratification. Perhaps, now he had the tiniest insight into the sort of relationship that some of his friends had found.

Chapter Nine

Tia sank back into the chair, leaving the book, still forgotten, lying at her feet. Her fingers drifted to her lips, feeling their slightly swollen tenderness, and she was aware of his taste still on her tongue, as she relived the memory of his arms about her, warming her through, as they drew her against his hard body.

Time passed, but Tia saw no point in moving. She wanted to treasure this moment as long as possible. She was still sitting there when the clock struck midnight, and Christmas Eve became Christmas.

Sighing, she rose, knowing that she should return to the ball, for supper would be served soon, and her Papa would worry if she was not there.

Straightening her dress, she smiled – for her Christmas wish had come true, and his kiss was the best Christmas present she could ever receive.

And then there was his promise to seek her out again. Suddenly, her world seemed full of potential... wonderful things could happen.

Tia hummed happily to herself as she went back to the Ballroom, already starting to imagine what might happen tomorrow.

Discover more about Lady Theodora in

'A Gift of Love' – a subscriber exclusive story, available free when you sign up for my newsletter at www.ariettarichmond.com/newsletter-signup/

and in Book 1 of the Derbyshire Set –

'The Earl's Unexpected Bride'

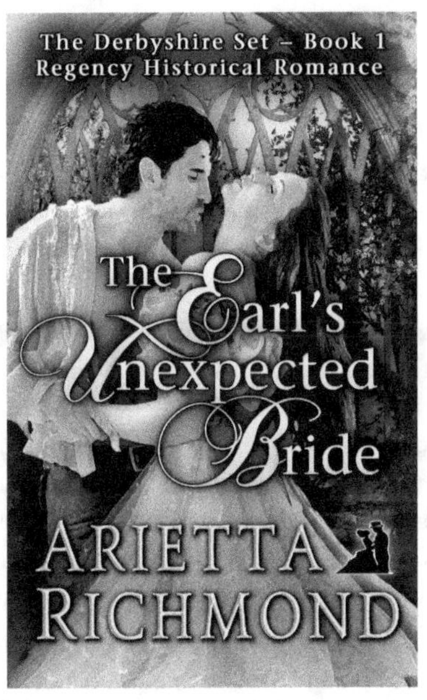

And also in the forthcoming Book 10 in the series

'The Duke's Improper Love'.

About The Author

Arietta Richmond has been a compulsive reader and writer all her life. Whilst her reading has covered an enormous range of topics, history has always fascinated her, and historical novels have been amongst her favourite reading.

She has written a wide range of work, from business articles and other non-fiction works (published under a pen name) but fiction has always been a major part of her life. Now, her Regency Historical Romance books are finally being released. The Derbyshire Set is comprised of 11 novels (9 released so far). The 'His Majesty's Hounds' series is comprised of 17 novels, with the last having just been released. The 'A Duke's Daughters – The Elbury Bouquet' series is comprised of seven books, with the second having just been released.

She also has a number of standalone novels, and four other series of novels in development. She lives in Australia, and when not reading or writing, likes to travel, and to see in person the places where history happened.

Be the first to know about it when Arietta's next book is released! Sign up to Arietta's newsletter at

http://www.ariettarichmond.com

When you do, you will receive two free subscriber exclusive books - **'A Gift of Love',** which is a prequel to the Derbyshire Set series, and ends on the day that 'The Earl's Unexpected Bride' begins, and **'Madame's Christmas Marquis'** which is an additional story in the His Majesty's Hounds series.

These stories are not for sale anywhere – they are absolutely exclusive to newsletter subscribers!

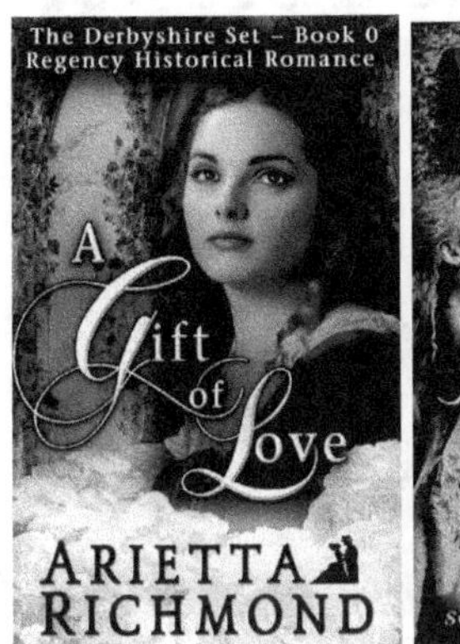

Connect with Arietta:

Follow her on Amazon - https://www.amazon.com/Arietta-Richmond/e/B016GG1KJ6/

Like her Facebook Page - https://www.facebook.com/AriettaRichmondAuthor

Follow her on Twitter - https://twitter.com/AriettaRichmond

Follow her on Instagram - https://www.instagram.com/AriettaRichmond/

Follow her on Bookbub – https://www.bookbub.com/authors/arietta-richmond

Follow her on Goodreads - https://www.goodreads.com/author/show/14508806.Arietta Richmond

Here is your preview of

Book One of the

Derbyshire Set series

Chapter One

As the water closed over her head, the events of the last few minutes replayed themselves in Catherine's mind, with the intense clarity that sometimes comes in dreams. But this was all too horribly real.

The water was such a cold shock after the warm sun of the bright May morning, and part of her believed that she would drown, even while she flailed against it.

She had been walking along the road from Lavenham to Harteston, returning from a visit to her mother's friend, Mrs Brown, when she first heard the sound of a horse's hooves.

Not those of just any horse she might have heard, picking its steady way along the hard-packed earth of the road, but a powerful, fast horse, obviously in some considerable hurry, hooves pounding out the urgency of its pace. It stopped her right in her tracks for a moment, so out of place was that rush on this quiet road.

The thudding rhythm, the pounding of its progress - she heard it coming up ahead of her, on the other side of the bridge, although she could not yet see it, for the trees and the high bank on the side of the road quite obscured what might lie around the corner.

She was, for no sensible reason, filled with a sudden dread - not a horrible sense of fear, or a real worry for her safety, but a dread nonetheless, at what was approaching, at the source of that clamour, coming towards her from around the corner.

Then, taking her first few steps onto the bridge over the Shimpling stream, she saw him. He came clattering onto the wooden slats of the bridge, apparently unconcerned by the prospect of any passer-by.

The first thing that struck her, in that first instant that she saw him, was the rider, his thighs, to be precise, inappropriate as that may be. He sat the horse with the confidence of long years riding, and controlled the stallion without apparent effort. His powerful thighs, flexing as they held him effortlessly in place, spoke eloquently of power and authority.

She was embarrassed by her thoughts, and a flush of colour came to her cheeks, but she could not drag her eyes away.

His breeches, creamy white and tight as skin, clung to him, giving definition to every muscle and sinew. His boots were almost as magnificent, well-worn black leather, the same colour as the horse's glistening hide.

Everything about him spoke of wealth and power.

He sat atop his animal with an easy grace, casual almost in his manner, unencumbered by a glove or a hat. From the other end of the bridge, she could take in all of his magnificence, the broad strong chest, the shoulders that seemed to span the entire width of the road, the chin that jutted forward. His face was strong, robust and masculine, with chiselled cheek-bones below dark eyes.

And on top of it all, above the square manliness of his face, and the rather wild look of his eyes, was a rich mane of dark hair, shot through with red and gold tones, that glinted in the sun, tousled, swept aside by the onrushing wind and lent buoyancy by an irrepressible energy that could be felt the moment you saw him.

She suspected that hair was not easily controlled. So focussed was she on the sight in front of her, that she had simply stopped walking, unaware that she had done so.

The horse did not stop as it came towards her. Its rider seemed not to see the small and simply dressed young woman on the bridge, who also had cause to cross the green expanse of the Shimpling stream, late this Thursday afternoon in May.

He spurred his mount on, charging over the rickety structure, as if he were master of all he surveyed.

She realised, with a gasp, that he was not going to stop for her, and, with a cry, threw herself to the side.

Almost brushing the stallion's flank, she hurled herself against the side rail, but could not stop herself from toppling, tumbling over the rickety rail and into the stream.

With an almighty splash, and a roaring in her ears, she was in the water. She could feel the slimy grasp of the reeds, feel the weight of all the water on top of her as she flailed about. She panicked.

She had never learned to swim. The mill pond at the back of her village school had always seemed too terrifying to enter, and she had never learned. The thoughts rushed through her mind, replaying, over and over, the last few minutes, as she desperately fought the water, all to no effect.

She grasped around for the bank, for something to cling onto, but nothing presented itself to her flailing hands. She could barely see in all the darkness of the stream, and could feel her dress and petticoats soaking up the water, weighing her down, pulling her to the rocky bed of the stream.

Every moment she became more certain that she was about to drown.

But then she felt something, a firm hand, a grasp from above, a man's grip. She was dragged up until she broke the surface of the water, spluttering uncontrollably.

Some heroic force hauled her onto the river bank, onto the dry grass just above the shore.

She was held in a standing position, only by the strength of her saviour's grip – he legs as yet refused to support her.

She looked up, still panting for breath. It was him. Of course it was him. Her assailant had become her saviour. He held her close, waiting to see if she could stand, if she would pull away.

Looking past his shoulder, she could see that the stallion was tied to a tree in the background, pawing at the grass, obviously wishing to be away and running again. She looked up into those dark devilish eyes and could not help but smile, even though her teeth chattered from the chill of the water.

"Are you quite all right?" he asked, with an uncertainty to his voice that betrayed his concern.

"Yes, yes quite all right." Her voice was shaky, and she was still short of breath, nerves still jangling from her watery encounter. She suspected, strongly, that she sounded unconvincing. Her eyes met his and she drank him in – he was just as good to look upon close up, as he had been from a distance.

"I must thank you kind sir, by your hand I appear to have been rescued from a watery grave."

"It was only because of me that you found yourself in such a predicament to begin with" he said, without hesitation.

His tone was that of man used to making declarations, to ordering the world around him. She realised that he held her slight frame in his embrace still, and could not but feel a shiver at the sensation.

She knew that she should pull away, should put distance between them, that this was highly inappropriate, yet she did not want to. It was pleasant, every once in a while to have a saviour this handsome.

She was not used to anyone else taking care of her, except her mother.

"I must apologise for my haste in crossing the bridge," he continued.

"It appears to have compromised your passage somewhat. I was, unfortunately, rather distracted — after a trying morning, I just wanted to ride, and ignore the world."

"Oh, not at all sir" she replied, (although it was patently obvious that he spoke the truth).

She was still shaky, and unable to find anything sensible to say - she had often struggled to maintain her composure around handsome gentlemen – in fact, she had very little experience with gentlemen at all. Regardless of the fact that he had caused her fall into the stream, her gratitude to him for saving her was immense, for surely, without him, she would have drowned.

"Please!" he cried, cutting her off. "Do not deny it, the fault was entirely mine."

He released her, apparently having finally noticed that they were in a rather inappropriate proximity to each other, and stepped back cautiously, watching to make sure that she could stand on her own. His immaculately tailored coat of bottle green superfine clung to his shoulders, quite as beautifully tailored as those breeches, and showing of his devastatingly well-made body. She was horrified to see that the fabric was marred by splashes of water, and that the pristine whiteness of his breeches had rather suffered from the muddiness of the stream. Yet she was shocked to realise that she felt a desire to be back in the embrace of those arms, it had made her feel safe, to be held so, and she could not but consider what might follow such an embrace.

Her breath hitched at the thought, and, as he looked at her, patiently waiting to see what she would do, his eyes still full of concern, she became conscious of her wetness, of how it must make her face red and shiny, of how her hair was clinging unflatteringly to the side of her head and of how her bodice was clinging rather revealingly to her body, the cloth made somewhat translucent by the water.

The light stays that she wore, and the somewhat old and thin state of the fabric of her gown, did little to conceal her figure, once totally soaked in the water of the stream. It brought a blush to her cheeks, but he did not look concerned.

"I must regretfully confess, I can often become rather distracted when I take my afternoon ride." As he spoke was looking over at the horse, gesturing.

She looked down, blushing, and ashamed of her state, and realised that he was wet up to his knees, his beautiful Hessians undoubtedly ruined.

He had waded into the stream to save her, compromised his own dignity for her safety - how remarkably unlike most of the noble gentlemen that she had met before (admittedly, there were not many). This, she allowed herself to think, was quite an unusual man.

That, she thought, following the line of his hand to the horse, was quite some animal. It would take a remarkable man to tame it.

She could not ride – a humble village girl had no chance or reason to learn – her feet, or the innkeepers cart, had always been enough for her. Yet she knew a quality horse when she saw one.

"I recently acquired this splendid mount" he waved to the horse once more "at an auction at Tattersalls. I was informed by my dealer, Mr. Redgrave, that he was bred in the stables of the Maharajah of Nackulpande, renowned as the greatest horse breeder in all of His Majesty's colonies".

He fixed his gaze back on her. "His studs are renowned for their power and virility. Thaddeus here came at a not inconsiderable expense, but I believe such extravagance to have been worthwhile."

She nodded, unfamiliar with such matters – she could tell that the horse was quality, but of what type, or to what extent, she had no idea.

She had never once ridden a horse herself.

"He is as powerful as he is headstrong. I see plenty of my own self in him – That is probably why we suit."

He looked back, when she made no response. She could think of nothing to say, she was too caught up in watching him, in the obvious energy that he brought to everything he did. It was compelling, and exciting.

He mistook her silence for disinterest.

"I pray I have not bored you with all of this discussion of the stallion. As an unmarried man, I am not often called upon to converse with ladies outside the confines of the drawing room and the ballroom. But where are my manners – here I am rambling on about my horse, and you are standing there, dripping wet and cold. Come, let me help you up the bank to the road."

He offered his hand. She clasped it, and felt a quaking in her breast, a quivering in the bottom of her stomach. He was unmarried! And so handsome and wealthy! How was it even possible? This chance encounter appeared to offer one of the great excitements of her life, and she could already feel her mind brimming with new passions, new hopes, new desires.

Village girls dreamed of things like this, of accidental meetings with handsome, wealthy noblemen, and, of course, those dreams always had a happy ending, with the couple falling in love.

She shook herself, mentally – this was reality, no dream, and the chances of anything happening were remote, to say the least.

"I thank you sir" she said, a little shakily, as she reached the top of the bank, and stepped on to the edge of the road. "And I must say that it is not at all tiresome to hear so eloquent an insight, on a subject with which I was not previously familiar."

"You flatter me" he said, with an ironic smile. "But I know enough of young ladies to have some awareness that the subject of stallions and auction houses does not generally greatly excite their interest."

He smiled and she could not help herself but smile warmly back. He had revealed another side, the tiniest hint of softness, of charm.

"Tell me miss, what is your name?" he enquired, with a renewed gravity.

His warmth was hidden again, tantalising her in the background.

She examined her feet humbly before she could look him once more in the eyes.

"My name is Catherine Thornberry."

"A charming name. The sweetness in the wilderness. I have always had a fondness for it." She blushed at this spontaneously poetic response.

"Allow me to introduce myself; I am Charles Rockingham, Earl of Stanningfield. I must confess that I am surprised to have stumbled upon you. I had presumed myself to be familiar with every pretty young lady in the county, but it appears that at least one had slipped my notice - and barely a mile from my own estate. Amusing is it not, how these things can pass us by?"

"Oh yes sir, indeed it is!" she said, in a rush, excited by his flattery.

The Earl of Stanningfield, here on Shimpling bridge, plucking her, Miss Catherine Thornberry, from the stream as if it were the most natural thing on earth! Catherine had a horrible suspicion that she was gushing, that she was making a fool of herself, but this man had an odd effect on her - she found that she struggled to think sensibly in his presence.

She was awestruck. Having never seen the Earl before, but having heard, from her friends and from her mother, much of his exploits, she had not anticipated that he should be so young, so handsome, so gallant in his readiness to help a young lady in distress.

The tales she had heard painted him as a rake, as a man with a great deal of life experience. She had expected an older man, heavy of body from overindulgence, and jaded in his attitude to life. Nothing could be further from the man who stood before her. She tried, as hard as she could, not to allow another red blush to flush her face, but it was all too much. It was all unreal, as if in a dream.

"Do not look so thunder-struck Miss Thornberry." He spoke forcefully - "You may have formed some idea of my reputation on the basis of idle parish gossip, but I must assure you that the overwhelming bulk of it is hearsay."

"I'm sure that it is sir, undoubtedly!" She was gushing again - it had always been a profound concern of hers that she came across as too enthusiastic in the presence of gentlemen. She checked herself.

"I have been at great pains to impress upon the county my courteous nature, but regrettably, I have an unfortunate past that seems to stalk me like a wolf."

She nodded gravely. She had heard some such stories, and always suspected that there might be some truth to them.

Nevertheless, being of a kind and trusting nature, she had always wanted to believe that they were false, or at least, misrepresented. She found that she did not want to believe this man capable of terrible things.

"We shall speak no more of such unpleasantness. Please, allow me to escort you homeward. It would be the least kindness I could offer after our unfortunate interaction on the bridge."

"Oh sir, that will not be necessary. I am quite capable of completing my journey unaccompanied."

"I insist" he said, not as a politeness, but a declaration. "You are shaking like a willow in a gale and as wet as a hunting dog, and all on my account. It would be most improper of me to abandon you here." His expression was serious as he spoke, and, again, she felt that the concern in his eyes was genuine.

"I will not have it said of me that I abandoned a fair and defenceless lady, drenched, on the side of the road. And besides" he added, with a glimmer in the corner of his rich brown eyes "what on earth would your neighbours say if I did?"

They shared a chuckle at his little joke.

"Thaddeus awaits!" laughing, he took her hand, tugging her towards the horse.

"But sir!" Catherine exclaimed "I regret to confess, I have never ridden before, and I do not know how!"

"Good heavens above!" he seemed genuinely shocked "Not ridden a horse? Why it is one of life's greatest pleasures! I would not wish to deny the thrill of a good, vigorous ride to my worst enemy. Allow me…"

Before Catherine even had time to make an objection, he had scooped her up.

She clasped his thick, muscular shoulders and found suddenly that her face was close to his, so close, in fact, that she could see every bristling hair, every tendon in his neck. Close inspection did him justice. His scent came to her, an earthy mixture of horse, leather, and an undertone of some more exotic scent, some cologne of citrus and spices. It was like nothing she had smelled before. She found it stimulating, and extremely pleasant.

"Time I think, for your first ride!" he chortled, before depositing her unceremoniously to sit sideways across Thaddeus' saddle. She felt the animal shifting beneath her, full of vigorous life.

She clung to the abundant mane that drifted back over her hands, holding on as if for dear life, anxious that the horse might suddenly take off without warning, or that it would deposit her once again into the stream.

It had a will of its own and a powerful body after all, but her saviour, the Earl, held firmly to its reins.

He gently stroked the horse's nose to calm it, putting it under his spell, before firmly commanding it to stand. Then in a single, graceful movement, he swung up into the saddle, lifting her to sit, still sideways, across his knees, his arms either side of her shaking body, and took charge of his stallion.

"Hold on tight" he declared, and she obeyed willingly.

There was a moment where she hesitated, aware that her soaking clothes were already shedding even more water onto his attire, before a movement of the horse convinced her that she was quite happy to sacrifice his clothing for her safety. She wrapped her white arms, still cold and wet, about his splendid torso, as tightly as she dared, her head resting against his shoulder. The shape and definition of his firm abdominal muscles could be made out beneath his coat and shirt.

The sensation quite took her breath away.

"Now where would you like me to take you, Miss Thornberry?" he asked, after a moment.

"To Hawthorn Cottage in Harteston" she replied. "Do you know it?"

"I know Harteston, but not the exact location of Hawthorn Cottage" he said. "A fine village indeed - do you live there alone?" As he spoke, without warning her, he had shifted Thaddeus into motion, and already they were crossing the bridge at a gentle canter. She was, again, impressed at his gallantry, as he was now heading the opposite way to his own original route.

With the unfamiliar rocking motion of the horse, and the stress of its forward motion pressing her ever more tightly against the body of her saviour, she could feel something thrilling stirring within her. A new sensation, pleasurable, dangerous, was creeping up her inner thighs and into her bosom. She bit the back of her lip. It was entirely inappropriate for her to be thinking such thoughts about this man.

He was far above her, he was courteous enough to have saved her from drowning, and here she was thinking like a wanton.

Well, she thought that's what it was – actually, she had no idea, no idea beyond the fact that her body was reacting to its proximity to his – and she was scandalously enjoying it.

"Or…" he continued with a roguish chuckle "have you a sweetheart in Harteston perhaps?" This time she was wise to him. This time she played the game.

"I am unmarried, my Lord. However…" she added, with a slight laugh of her own "I must confess that the innkeeper's son and I have developed something of a rapport in recent times. He is a most handsome young man."

"Oh undeniably" replied the Earl, rising to her challenge. "Indeed I have often thought to myself, on visiting that very fine inn, that he would make a most attractive catch for a young girl in the village. Nevertheless", He paused in his speech a moment, as if considering the right words to use. Thaddeus was picking up speed. Her lower body was assailed with a new vigour, rocked against the Earl's thighs, and the front of his body, in a rather intimate fashion.

The warmth of his body was penetrating the chill of her wet clothes – it made her want to press herself even closer against him.

Having obviously chosen his words carefully, he continued "Are his manners and breeding not a little coarse, for a young lady of distinction, such as yourself?"

Catherine did not allow herself to laugh, but she was overwhelmed. This man was clever. He knew the workings of the female heart. Moreover, by asking this question, which she now, perforce, had to answer, he had coaxed a difficult admission out of her, concerning their relative status.

"I am but a humble schoolmistress, sir" she said reluctantly. "I have education and, I flatter myself, a little breeding – but certainly not any significant status in the world."

"Stuff! I could tell the moment that I saw you, that here is a lady who carries herself well, evident poverty notwithstanding."

"You are indeed, courteous, my Lord. Nevertheless, I could never make any claims to be a noble lady. My mother, with whom I share Hawthorn Cottage, has long maintained that we are descended from the de Quincy family, who came over with William the Conqueror no less, but I fear, from what little she is willing to tell me of the detail, that lineage may be rather obscure now, to say the least."

"The de Quincys?" he came back, not bothering to disguise how impressed he was. "Not bad at all. Tell me, how does a girl with such a fine pedigree find herself reciting the alphabet to ungrateful village brats?"

"I suppose some ancestor of ours must have fallen on hard times" she said, keeping her poise.

Thaddeus was going at quite a speed now, and it was necessary to raise her voice. She tried as hard as she dared to disguise the quaking in her body that the movement of the ride, and the sensation of his body against hers, was giving her.

"Mother has mentioned a gambler, in my great grandmother's generation, who may have lost us our estates. That is long ago, and of no relevance to our lives now. I am unused to luxury, and the life of a humble schoolmistress is easy enough to bear."

He had exposed a quiet sadness in her, a longing.

For years she had ignored her mother's pining after their heritage, her obsession with the importance of ancestors on their family tree, but now, in the presence of a real gentleman, she was, for the first time, embarrassed by her circumstances. She had no land, no money, no prospects of a higher match.

All she had ever hoped for was to make an honest living and to marry one of the boys in the village, but now, something else had stirred in her, passion, ambition, a reaching for something more. Thaddeus' movement seemed to fill her with a greater lust for more in life, as well as most interesting sensations in her body, with every galloping stride.

"I suppose someone's got to force some knowledge into 'em," he laughed, urging the horse along.

The countryside sped by. She took in long, drooping willows, plump cows chomping in the fields, water mills churning, as they had for hundreds of years. It was not such bad country, Suffolk, especially as it had such charming people in it. The speed at which the road went by amazed her, so used was she to the time it took to walk this distance.

"Still, it is a terrible shame for a great and noble family to have fallen on hard times. Alright, I suppose, if you're happy enough looking after other people's infants, and cavorting with innkeepers' sons, then I can think of worse fates."

"Why yes sir. I suppose I am happy enough." She knew, even as the words came out, that she was lying to him.

Had someone asked her the question yesterday, then that answer would have been truthful, but today, she was alarmed to discover, something in her had changed. She was no longer satisfied with what she had.

"Well, jolly good then."

He appeared to focus his concentration on riding now, for the first time taking his attention away from her. She could not help but feel a small pang of disappointment.

Thaddeus thundered on, down a shallow hill, and then splashed across a ford. Before she knew it, having never ridden upon a horse or experienced just quite how fast these noble animals could move, she was in the village of Harteston, shaken by the journey, quivering and awake deep in her body, and intensely aware of his body where it pressed against her.

"Here we are" he declared confidently. "Harteston - where I suppose I shall leave you."

"Yes. I must thank you my Lord, your kindness has saved me much effort, and possibly even preserved my life. For surely, had I not drowned, by now I would have taken a terrible chill on the road home."

"No need to thank me Miss Catherine, I am sure that you would have done the same were our roles to be reversed."

"I suppose I would have. Thank you again."

She released her grip on his body, regretfully, and he lifted her gently, supporting her as she slid down the side of the horse to land on her feet.

She hesitated, unsure of what to do now, part of her not wishing this moment to end, but unable to see any reason for it to continue. Then, not wishing to betray the feelings that he had stirred in her, and holding her crumpled bonnet high upon her head, she dipped him a curtsey, and set off for home.

The Earl however, had never been the kind to let a pretty young lady get away from him, so coldly and suddenly. As she had silently, privately hoped, he swung out of his saddle and came straight after her, catching her in just a few steps.

Grasping her fragile waist, he turned her suddenly towards him.

She gasped, her eyes wide open. He pulled her against him, and the heat of his body against hers felt like fire rushing through her veins.

"Not so fast" he whispered, close against her ear. "We haven't even said a proper goodbye" and then, just like that, he kissed her, fully, without apology, on the lips.

He gripped her for a moment that felt like it should last forever, a moment deserving of a painting or a symphony to capture it and preserve it. She felt his strong tongue, his hot mouth and his firm lips. Their bodies pressed together, seeming moulded just for that, and she could sense the longing they shared could feel the hardness of his desire, tangible through their damp clothing. Her body throbbed, with the sensation of the kiss, and the vitality imparted by the ride.

Just as suddenly as he had captured her, he pulled back, looking a little shocked himself, at what he had just done. He mumbled goodbye, and swung back into the saddle, heading for home.

Catherine stood a moment, dazed, watching him go. She had never felt such a thrill in all of her twenty-four years on God's earth.

Charles Rockingham, Earl of Stanningfield, was bemused. He rather feared that he had just made a fool of himself, in front of a young lady. Not something that he had ever been prone to doing. *That is,* an insidious thought reminded him, *except for the colossal fool he had made of himself, at 17, with Monique.*

He pushed the thought aside. That was old history, beyond being changed. Today, he should be focussing on his current problems. And what problems. He groaned as it all forced itself back to the surface of his mind, now that he no longer had a ready distraction to hand.

He chose to shove the thoughts away again, an act made easy by the fact that his clothes were uncomfortably damp, and his toes squished alarmingly in his boots, which were, he suspected, full of water.

They were certainly coated in mud. The condition of his attire would draw the wrath of his valet, and he expected that Johnson would be effective at making his disapproval known, without ever saying a word.

Still, even if he had rather made a fool of himself, it was, he decided, worth it. He had been in such a temper when he had left the house. His morning, reading through applications for the role of Theodora's Governess, had been enough to drive anyone to despair.

They were, universally, terrible. The sort of women he would definitely never want in his house – the sort who would turn a bright, if sometimes difficult, girl into a prudish, boring society Miss, incapable of conversing on any topic except the weather.

He knew that the best solution to such a mood was a good hard ride, on a quality horse. And Thaddeus was quite the best horse that he had ever owned.

But it had been spectacularly unwise of him to ride, at that pace, along the road – over the fields would have been a far better choice.

Well too late to change anything now. And…. Would he want to?

The girl was beautiful – and, it seemed, completely unaware of that fact. He had not seen her, not until it was too late. He had been so wrapped in his thoughts that the world around him had been barely registering.

He might not have seen her, but the thump against his leg as he rode across the bridge, followed by the scream, and the huge splash, had certainly attracted his attention.

At that point he had no idea who or what he had just caused to fall into the Shimpling Stream, beyond the fact that it was almost certainly a person, as nothing else screamed quite like that. Unwilling to leave anyone floundering due to his inattention, he had hauled Thaddeus around (somewhat against the stallions wishes at the time!) and gone back to investigate.

What he dragged from the water was a delectable surprise.

A girl, or young woman rather, her shape thoroughly displayed by the unfortunate saturation of her gown, her piercing blue eyes shocking in her pale, water-soaked face, her sodden hair seemingly a golden-brown colour – although the mud made it hard to tell. She had blushed charmingly as he held her, waiting for her to be steady on her feet again.

She held herself well – there was obviously some breeding there, or at least some education, but the gown was, as far as he could tell after its dip in the stream, rather worn. It had been good quality once, but the hems showed signs of it having been turned, and the fabric was thin from wear. Thinness he deeply appreciated, as it ensured that the water had made it almost translucent. It had taken all his concentration to avoid staring at her breasts rather than her face.

Apart from the sodden gown, and its exposure of her attractions, there was something about her that took his breath away, in that first look.

It took only a moment to realise what – her shape, the turn of her cheek, the fall of her hair, even sodden, brought to mind, just for a second, Monique. He had pushed that recognition away, and focussed on her more mundane attractions.

He had been a rake for too many years not to appreciate a woman's body when he was given an unexpected viewing. But it seemed that he was rather out of practice.

The sight of her body had robbed him of sensible, coherent conversation, and he had made a complete ass of himself, prattling on at her about the horse, of all things. Women, in his experience, did not give a damn about horses, so long as they transported them where they wanted to go. He was depressingly sure that he could not have made a bigger fool of himself if he had tried.

And then, to top it off, he had taken her home. What else could a gentleman do? He certainly couldn't leave her to walk four miles in a soddenly transparent dress, when she was already shivering from the cold! What if she had met some oaf along the way, who thought to take advantage of her? *Like you wanted to,* said that insidious voice in his thoughts. She was schoolmistress at the parish school — the school that his family funded, had funded for 50 years now, for the good of their tenants and the villagers. A less suitable woman for him to find tempting he couldn't imagine.

The feel of her body against him, of her arms around him and her soft breasts pressed against his chest, rubbing against him with the movement of the horse, the feel of her rounded derriere, rubbing against his thighs, pressing against his manhood, had been enough to drive a saint wild.

The wet fabric of her gown was no barrier, and the water soon transferred to his breeches as well. They might as well have been skin to skin, he could feel the detail of her body so clearly.

His cock had hardened in response, making the ride an exquisite agony. She must be an innocent, for she had appeared to genuinely not notice, even though Thaddeus' every stride had thrust the evidence of his arousal against her nether regions.

Which made his behaviour at the end of the ride all the more despicable.

Not only had he flirted with her, in a rather suggestively inappropriate way, but he had, at the end, kissed her…. Hard…. Full on the lips. He had not intended to, but, when she turned away, all stiff and unsure, after that ever so wobbly curtsey, and simply began to walk off, her ridiculously crushed and sodden bonnet perched on her equally sodden hair, he had not been able to stop himself.

He wanted a reaction, wanted more than just a departure.

He did not know why - he was, obviously, simply a fool. But he had gone after her, grabbed her and pulled her to him. In the middle of the damned village street, for pity's sake! And she had tasted divine. Her innocent response had been to press into the kiss, and the feel of her body fitting so perfectly against his had roused his passion like no woman had for years. Had the chiming of the town clock not interrupted, he might almost have taken her there, on the street. He was, most definitely, a fool.

And, he was no further ahead with solving the governess problem.

He was just as frustrated by that as before, but now, he was frustrated in an entirely different way, and sodden as well. He sighed, and steeled himself for Johnson's response to his maltreatment of his attire.

Read the rest at

https://www.amazon.com/dp/B01FJEQPXM

Books in The Derbyshire Set

The Earl's Unexpected Bride

The Captain's Compromised Heiress

The Viscount's Unsuitable Affair

The Count's Impetuous Seduction

The Rake's Unlikely Redemption

The Marquess' Scandalous Mistress

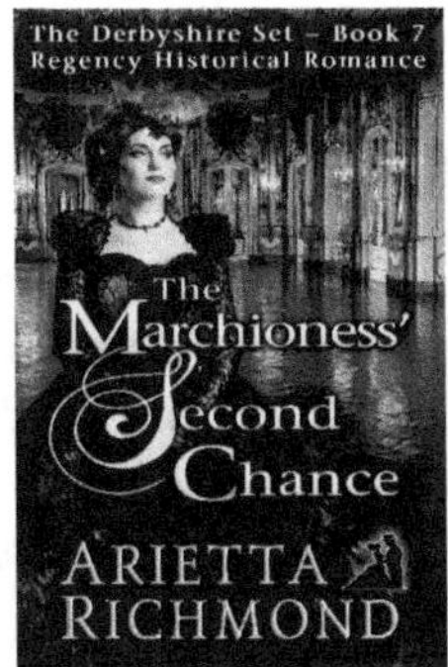

The Marchioness' Second Chance

Lady Theodora's Christmas Wish

A Viscount's Reluctant Passion

The Derbyshire Set Omnibus Edition Vol. 1 (the first three books all in one)

The Derbyshire Set Omnibus Edition Vol. 2 (the second three books all in one)

Books in the His Majesty's Hounds Series

<u>Claiming the Heart of a Duke</u>

<u>Intriguing the Viscount</u>

<u>Giving a Heart of Lace</u>

<u>Being Lady Harriet's Hero</u>

<u>Enchanting the Duke</u>

<u>Redeeming the Marquess</u>

<u>Finding the Duke's Heir</u>

<u>Winning the Merchant Earl</u>

<u>Healing Lord Barton</u>

<u>Kissing the Duke of Hearts</u>

<u>Loving the Bitter Baron</u>

<u>Falling for the Earl</u>

<u>Rescuing the Countess</u>

<u>Betting on a Lady's Heart</u>

<u>Attracting the Spymaster</u>

<u>Courting a Spinster for Christmas</u>

<u>Restoring the Earl's Honour</u>

Books in the A Duke's Daughters – the Elbury Bouquet Series

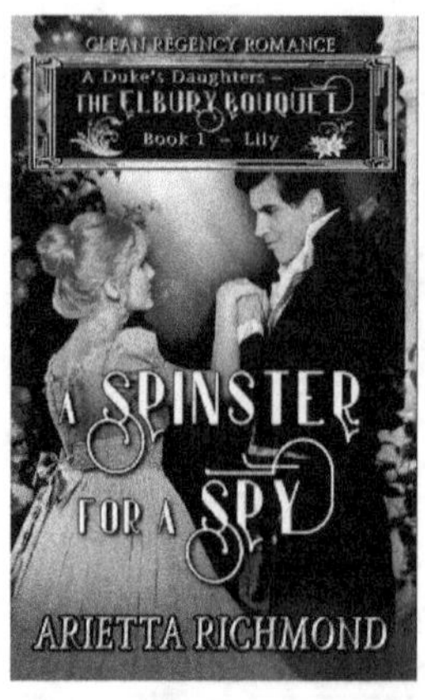

A Diamond for a Duke (Camellia)
(coming soon)
A Minx for a Merchant (Primrose)
(coming soon)
An Enchantress for an Earl (Violet)
(coming soon)
A Maiden for a Marquess (Iris)
(coming soon)
A Heart for an Heir (Thorne)
(coming soon)

Books in the Nettlefold Chronicles

Regency Collections with Other Authors

Other Books from Arietta

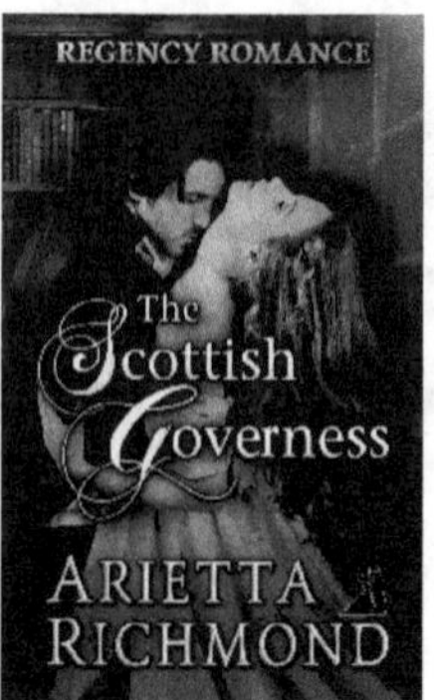

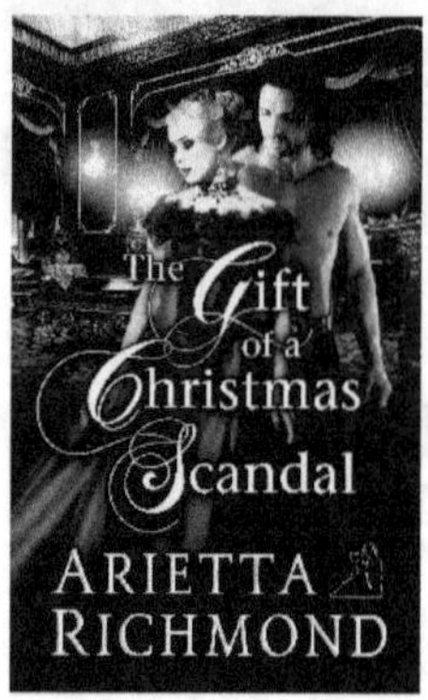

Other Books from Dreamstone Publishing

Dreamstone publishes books in a wide variety of categories, ranging from Erotica and Romance to Kids Books, Books on Writing, Business Books, Photography, Cook Books, Diaries, Coloring books and much more. New books are released each month.

Be the first to know when our next books are coming out

Be first to get all the news – sign up for our newsletter at

http://www.dreamstonepublishing.com